BOOK 3

Supermaths

Sue Atkinson

age 3-6

The fun, easy way to teach your child maths

Illustrated by **Ian Cunliffe**

Consultant: **Shirley Clarke**

Contents

Hodder Children's Books

a division ████████████ Limited

Why *Supermaths*?

Many adults fear maths because they feel that they were badly taught at school and are anxious not to pass their worries on to their children. But maths can be great fun!

Supermaths shows you how to teach maths to your child in an enjoyable way that will make him or her confident with the early maths that is taught at school.

A good attitude to maths has been shown to improve a child's motivation and achievement – so smile and praise their work. Above all – enjoy it!

How does *Supermaths* work?

Often children can count by rote and on their fingers by the time they go to school, but they lack the underlying skills and understanding of the early maths concepts. It is these "building blocks" that *Supermaths* provides so that the maths taught at school is built on a very secure foundation.

There are five books in the series. The *Supermaths* key skills on the inside front cover show which stages of early maths are taught in each book. Each book builds on the skills already learned and there are plenty of opportunities for revision and practice.

Each book is divided into six two-page units that centre on a rhyme, story, activity or game which forms the basis for the maths activities.

This is a double-page spread from Book 3.

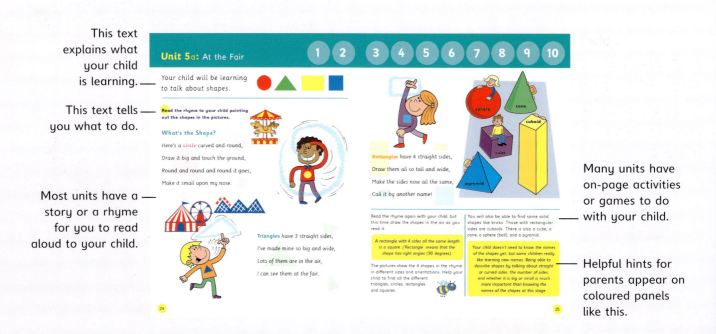

How do I know it will work?

Sue Atkinson has worked extensively with 3-6 year olds (and with early years teachers) and using the methods in this book the children she taught became visibly more confident in maths and "at home" with numbers.

I'm not a teacher – will I be able to do it?

Yes! **Supermaths** is clearly structured and clearly written in plain English with the main aspects of early maths repeated often enough for your child to understand thoroughly. In many ways parents are excellent teachers for their children as they know their children best and are working in a relaxed atmosphere at home.

I'm very busy – how much time will it take up?

If you spend about 10 minutes on **Supermaths** each day, your child will make good progress. Many of the activities can be done as a part of your daily life. For example, teaching your child weights and measures as you prepare a meal.

Can you find my 12 friends?

Buzzy Bees
There are 12 Buzzy Bees hidden in the book for your child to discover and count.

What items do I need to collect before we can start?

All you need are crayons or felt tip pens, a pencil and paper clip for the spinner, items to count (e.g. raisins, buttons, coins), scrap paper or card, and scissors.

Will *Supermaths* enable my child to do the Baseline tests at school?

All aspects of Baseline testing and nursery and reception maths for 3, 4 and 5 year olds are covered in this series. The later books introduce maths for 6 and 7 year olds as well, which will give your child a head start for the daily Numeracy Hour.

Each book is planned around the maths Early Learning Goals for the Foundation Stage. These are goals that most 4 and 5 year olds are expected to achieve by the time they finish in their reception year (primary 1 in Scotland), and cover counting, calculating, shape, space and measures.

How to use the spinner.

You will need a spinner to play some of the games. Position a pencil and a paper clip on the circle printed on the page (as shown here). Flick the paper clip with your finger to make it spin round the pencil tip.

Play this game often with your child at any stage in the book.

Rules:
1. Start with a counter each on the house.
2. Take turns to spin the spinner and move that many spaces along the track. If you land on a red star you can move on 5 more spaces.
3. The winner is the first player to reach the fun fair.

You need: a counter each, and a pencil and paper clip for the spinner (see page 3 for instructions).

30

29

28

27

26

25

24

23

22

21

20

19

18

17

16

15

14

13

12

11

10

9

8

7

6

5

4

3

2

1

Start

6 1 5 2 4 3

The Enormous Turnip

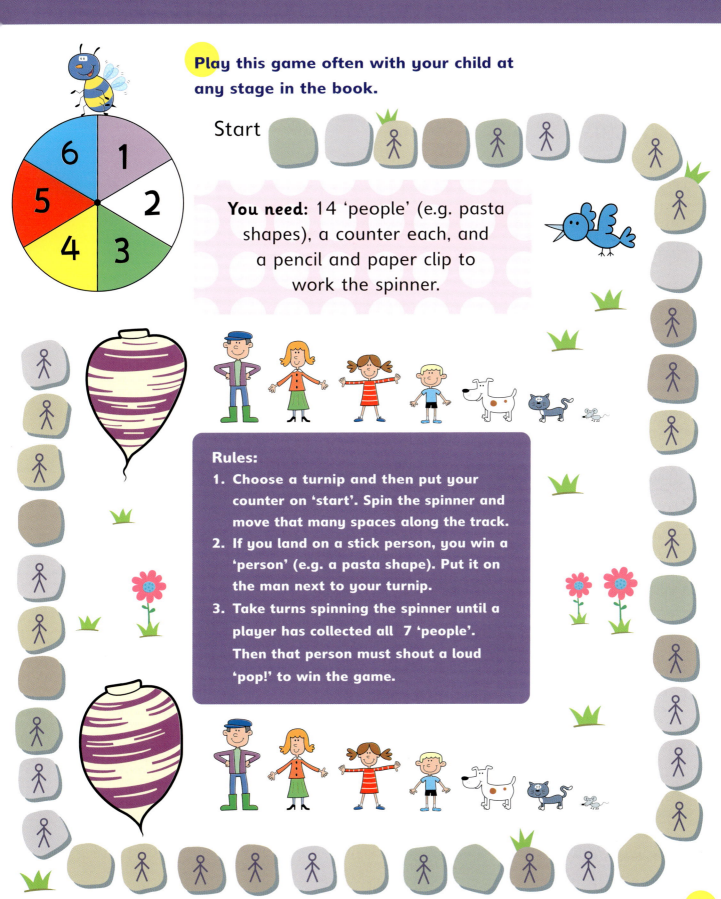

Play this game often with your child at any stage in the book.

Start

You need: 14 'people' (e.g. pasta shapes), a counter each, and a pencil and paper clip to work the spinner.

Rules:
1. Choose a turnip and then put your counter on 'start'. Spin the spinner and move that many spaces along the track.
2. If you land on a stick person, you win a 'person' (e.g. a pasta shape). Put it on the man next to your turnip.
3. Take turns spinning the spinner until a player has collected all 7 'people'. Then that person must shout a loud 'pop!' to win the game.

Your child will be learning to count 7 objects and know that the number remains the same even when the objects are moved.

Read the rhyme together several times.

As I Was Going to St Ives

As I was going to St Ives I met a man with **7** wives.

Each wife had **7** sacks,

Each sack had **7** cats,

Each cat had **7** kits,

Kits, cats, sacks and wives,

How many were going to St Ives?

Count the 7 wives in the picture and hold up 7 fingers to count. Help your child to count the 7 sacks that each wife has and to establish that there are lots of sacks altogether.

Find and count the cats and kittens in the picture. (There are 12 cats and 4 kittens to find.) Establish that there are 7 cats in each sack and therefore there are lots more cats than we can see. Say:

Shut your eyes and pretend you can see 7 cats inside each sack. There are even more cats than there are sacks and there are even more kittens than cats!

You could count out 7 building bricks to represent the cats in one sack and give each cat 7 kittens (buttons or raisins). If your child is just at the stage of counting out groups of 7, that is fine. If she is ready for more, help her to count all the cats in the sacks to see how far she can count. Join in with her counting by saying:

What a lot of cats and kittens! In each sack there are 7 cats and 49 kittens, so altogether there are 56 cats and kittens in just 1 sack!

Children usually enjoy playing with large numbers so let your child explore them if she wants to. You could say '100 and one more is 101', and then ask your child to do the same for a thousand, a million and a billion.

A calculator can also be ideal for having fun with large numbers.

Try to answer the question 'How many are going to St Ives?'. You could say that it is a trick question because it might have been just the speaker going to St Ives. The man, the wives, the cats and the kittens might have been going somewhere else!

Help your child to count out 7 counters and put one on each of the wives. Ask your child:

How many counters are there? Now move the counters and put them on the flowers on the grass over here. Are there still 7 counters?

*Don't be surprised if your child counts the counters from 1 again to see if there are still 7! As you work through the **Supermaths** books, she will come to understand that moving objects doesn't change the total number of objects.*

MORE THINGS TO TRY

Language and understanding of maths is very important in a child's development, so try to use words such as 'more', 'less' and 'fewer' whenever you can. For example:

If I get out another bowl, will I have more bowls or fewer bowls? We need less water than that in the vase.

The word 'fewer' seems to be particularly difficult for children to grasp so focus on this in particular by saying:

There are fewer sweets in my bag than yours. The baby has fewer candles on her cake than you.

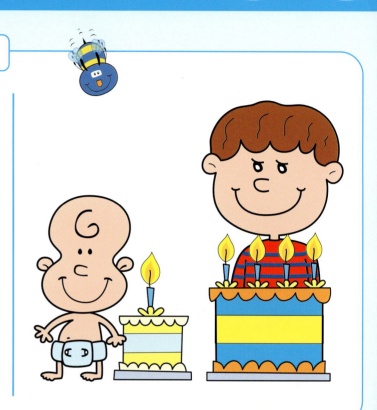

Keep counting! •

- Repeat the activity of counting out a few items at a time e.g. 6 spoons for breakfast. Then move them and ask your child:

  Are there still 6 spoons?

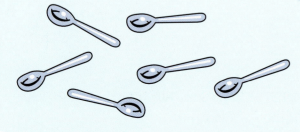

Be aware that children will often say the last option you give them e.g. If you ask them whether there are 6 or 7 spoons, they will probably say 7. Also, children often think that the total number must have changed, otherwise, why would you have asked the question!

- Count by rote (reciting the number names in order) to 10. If your child is confident with numbers, move on to 20, 50, and above.

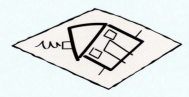

Maths fun!

Play the 'Race to the Fair' game on page 4.

You could make a number track on the floor from bits of scrap paper numbered 1 to 10, or if they feel confident with numbers, to 15 or 20. Make a house shape for zero. You could make the numbers into bear paw prints and your child could pretend to be one of The Three Bears as he takes steps along the track.

Ask your child to stand on the house and then to take a step forward to stand on 1, then another step to stand on 2 and so on, saying the numbers out loud. Make sure he just says one number word for each step.

Stepping along a number track like this is a 'multi-sensory experience', i.e. his foot moves as he hears you say the word and he says the word as well. Doing this activity is particularly important if your child has trouble counting objects accurately.

Number tracks and lines are used extensively in schools as they help children to develop an understanding of numbers.

Playing cards are a great way to develop your child's mathematical thinking. Play 'Pairs' by turning over 12 cards and finding different ways to pair them up. For example, the 4 of hearts could go with the 4 of spades. When you have found all the possible pairs you can turn over another 12 cards and continue the game.

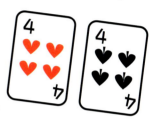

If your child is confident with numbers, you could choose a target number such as 7 and make pairs that add up to 7 e.g. the 5 of hearts with the 2 of clubs.

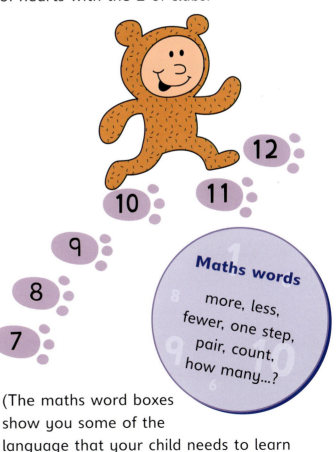

Maths words

more, less, fewer, one step, pair, count, how many...?

(The maths word boxes show you some of the language that your child needs to learn gradually in this book.)

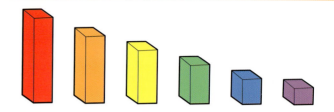

Your child will be learning to put things in order.

Read the story to your child pointing out the characters.

The Enormous Turnip

Once upon a time in a land not that far away, there lived a farmer who was a champion turnip grower. One day, when he tried to pull up a turnip to make turnip stew, he found that the turnip was so big that although he pulled with all his might, the turnip just wouldn't come up.

So the farmer called to his wife, "Come and help me pull up this enormous turnip so I can make a turnip stew."

Not another one of his revolting turnip stews, thought the wife, but there wasn't much else to eat so she went over and started helping him to pull.

Now there were 2 pulling and they pulled and pulled with all their might, but still the turnip didn't come up. So the wife called to her daughter to come and help.

I'm really busy inventing a way to get to the moon, thought the daughter, but I'd better go and help.

Now there were 3 people pulling and they pulled and pulled and pulled with all their might, but still the turnip didn't come up. So the daughter called to her little brother to come and help.

I'm trying to race these snails along this post, thought the boy, but I'd better help or mum might make me tidy my room.

Now there were 4 pulling and they pulled and pulled and pulled and pulled with all their might, but still the turnip didn't come up.

"We need more help," said the daughter, who was always very practical and knew how to solve problems. "Let's ask Jessie the dog to come and help."

Humans are so silly, thought Jessie. None of them likes turnip stew anyway, but I'd better go and help or they might make me eat some of it.

Now there were 5 pulling and they pulled and pulled and pulled and pulled and pulled with all their might, but still the turnip didn't come up.

What they need is to get that monstrous little cat to come and help, thought Jessie the dog, and she called the cat.

How stupid humans and dogs are, thought the cat, but if I help I might get to sit by the warm fire tonight.

Now there were 6 pulling and they pulled and pulled and pulled and pulled and pulled and pulled with all their might, but still the turnip didn't come up.

Then the mouse came out of her house in the barn and watched them all. "You're doing it all wrong," she said. "You have to pull like this." So she pulled, and they all pulled and suddenly, "POP!" out came the enormous turnip!

"Wonderful!" said the farmer. "Now I'll make turnip stew for everyone."

"How lovely," they all said. But they thought, oh no!

Read the story again, but this time use the character cards cut out or photocopied from page 5. As you read the story, encourage your child to put the cards in order:

First comes the man and next comes his wife, then their daughter. That's 3 people. If we add the little boy that's 4 people. Next comes the dog and the cat. That's 6 people and animals altogether.

MORE THINGS TO TRY

On the back of the number cards on page 6 are clowns in order of size. Lay the cards out flat and order them from the tallest to the shortest. Say:

This one is taller than that one. This one is the shortest. This one is the tallest.

Keep counting!

- Repeat the number track activity from unit 1, making sure that your child says just one number word for each step. Then start at the largest number and count back to zero.

Your child might not be able to lay down the track in order just yet, but keep practising. Being able to order numbers to 10 and above is a crucial skill your child will need for school.

- Put the number cards from page 5 in order. You could just focus on 1 to 7 at first and gradually add the other numbers as your child becomes more confident. You can add zero when your child has had plenty of experience counting along a number track. If he is ready to count beyond 10, just make more cards out of an old cereal box.

- If your child is quite confident with ordering numbers, race each other to lay down a set of ordinary playing cards in order from the ace to 10.

Maths **f**un!

Play 'The Enormous Turnip' game on page 7.

Emphasise to your child how things often have to be done in a particular order e.g. cooking beans:

1. open the tin

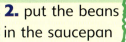

2. put the beans in the saucepan

3. heat the beans

4. put them on a plate

5. eat them

Ask your child 'What do we do next?' at each stage and then ask 'What do we do last?'.

Order other routines such as making toast, eating a bowl of cereal, starting the car, etc. When ordering your routine of starting the car say:

First we open the door and get in. Next we put our seat belts on. Then I put the key in the lock and turn it. The engine starts, and off we go!

1. open the door and get in

2. put on our seatbelts

3. put the key in lock and turn it

4. and off we go!

Maths words

next, order, beside, taller than, tallest, shortest, big, add, altogether, size, count

15

Unit 3a: Big Hug!

Your child will be learning to read and count numbers to 8.

Read the rhyme to your child several times, pointing to the numbers as you go along.

The Hugging Rhyme

1 tiny mouse,

2 big cats,

3 heavy elephants,
   all wearing hats.

4 tall giraffes,

5 long snakes,

6 small kangaroos,
   all baking cakes.

7 fat porcupines,

8 short slugs,
   always remember,
   give lots of big hugs!

Read the rhyme again, but this time count the animals in the pictures as you go along. Say:

Are there more cats than elephants? How many more? How many snakes are there? How many slugs are there?

Make sure that your child knows that when 'how many?' is asked, an appropriate response is to count the objects.

Make sure your child knows that the last number in the count is the total number in the set. If she counts 8 objects but then says there are 9, just reinforce the count to 8 again. There are many more times to practise this as you work through the books.

Look at the words for size in the rhyme, e.g. the slugs are short but the snakes are long. Ask:

Can you think of something else that is long?

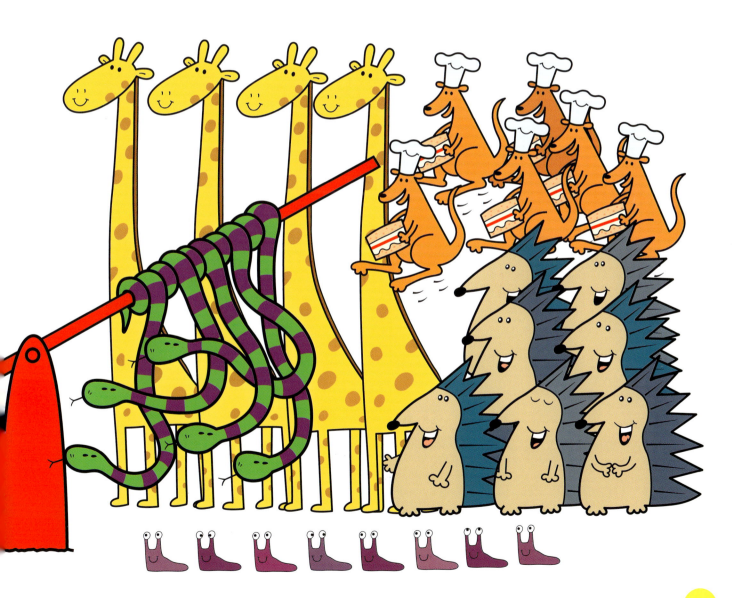

Pots and Beans

You need: 5 empty yogurt pots, dried beans, tape, a pencil, and paper.

Rules:
1. Put 0-4 beans in each of the 5 pots so that one pot has no beans, the next has 1 bean, another has 2 beans, and so on.
2. Count the beans with your child. Then turn the pots upside down and mix them up.
3. Ask your child to find the pot with 3 beans. It's hard because there are no labels on the pots, but it is a good way to build his attention skills.

Play the game a second time, but this time label each pot. Let your child draw something on the label to represent the number of beans in the pot.

Using conventional figures for numbers really isn't important at this stage, although it is great if your child does use them!

Hopefully he will be able to identify the right pots. This indicates that your child understands that symbols can have meaning and that they are essential for reading books, learning to write and to do maths. Celebrate with a big hug!

6 in the Pot

Rules:
1. Put 6 beans on the table and count them.
2. Ask your child to shut his eyes while you hide a few of the beans under a pot, leaving just a few to be counted.
3. Ask your child to open his eyes and count the beans he can see. He then has to work out how many beans are under the pot.
4. To vary the game, change over roles.

This is the beginning of adding and subtracting so extend the language as much as you possibly can.

Keep counting! • • • • • • • • • • • • •

- Cut out or photocopy the cards on page 5 and ask your child to match the 3 dots to the number 3 card, and the 2 dots to the number 2 card, etc. If he is confident with numbers, match the 10 dots with the 10 card. Ask:

  Which has the same number on both sides of the card? (The number 5 card.)

- Put about 6 objects (e.g. toys, bricks) in a circle and ask your child to count them.

It is quite usual for a child at this stage to forget where they started and to go on counting around the circle, past their starting point. Repeat with other numbers and different objects over the next few weeks, emphasising how important it is when we are counting to remember where we started.

Maths fun!

Finger Wizz!

Rules:
1. Both players put one hand behind their back and on the count of 3, they bring one hand to the front with any number of fingers up that they choose.
2. Count the number of fingers together.

Your child is likely to want to count the fingers from 1 each time, but gradually he will learn to see a certain number of fingers, put that figure in his head, and then add on the rest of the fingers. Say:

There are 3 fingers here, and 4 more here. Keep the number 3 in your head and then count on, 4, 5, 6 and 7. There are 7 fingers altogether.

This is quite an advanced stage and it will need to be developed gradually over a few days or weeks.

Maths words
more, less, big, small, tall, long, short, count, how many...?

Your child will be learning to understand ordinal numbers such as 1st, 2nd, 3rd, etc. and to use words for size and position.

Look at the clowns in the race and talk about them with your child:

Who is 1st in the race? What is that clown wearing? Who ran the fastest? Who ran the slowest? Who is just behind that clown? Describe the 2nd clown to me. Who is next? Point to the 3rd clown. Who is taller, the 3rd or the 4th clown? Put a bean on the 5th clown. What is the 7th clown wearing? Which clown is the shortest? and so on.

Count along the line of clowns with your child and ask her to count how many clowns are in the race.

Play 'I spy' with your child using the picture below. Describe something on one of the clowns and ask her to work out which clown you are describing. For example, say:

I spy 2 round buttons. I spy a tall hat. I spy a stripy hat. I spy a clown taller than the one with a very long tie.

You can reverse roles to add a little variety to the game.

MORE THINGS TO TRY

Find the Mouse

You need: different pots (e.g. beakers or mugs), small toys, buttons or beads.

Rules:
1. Put the pots in a line and decide which end of the line is going to be the start.
2. Ask your child to shut his eyes while you hide a small object under one of the pots.
3. Give him directions to find the object:

   The mouse is hiding under the pot next to the blue pot. The blue button is under the pot next to the 4th pot. The building brick is next but one to the 2nd pot.

Reverse roles if you are losing your child's attention to add a bit of variety to the game.

Keep counting! •

Count by rote to 30 with your child. (Just saying the numbers in the right order at this stage is fine, even if he can't count out that many objects accurately.)

28, 29 ,30!

Once counting to 30 is established, your child will start to see the patterns in the language of the numbers beyond 20 (e.g. 21, 22... 31, 32... etc.) Moving on to counting to 100 is not as difficult as it might sound. Just give lots of practice, e.g. by counting to 100 on the way to school.

Maths fun!

Race You!

You need: a counter each, and a pencil and paper clip for the spinner.

Rules:
1. Put a counter each on 'start' and take turns to spin the spinner. Move that many spaces along the track.
2. The first player to finish the game is the winner!

Variation: make the game harder by saying that you have to spin the exact number to get to the finish.

Check that your child is counting forwards and backwards correctly, taking one step for each number counted. Be aware that some children tend to say '1', but stay on the space they are on!

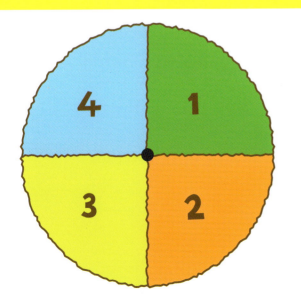

Start

1

2 Trip over. Move back 1.

3 Move on 2.

4 Sit and have a rest. Miss a go.

7 Stop for a drink of water. Miss a go.

6 Move back 1.

5

8 Bump into an elephant. Miss a go.

9

Finish

10 You are 1st.

Maths words

next, last, fastest, slowest, tallest, shortest, fattest, thinnest, forwards, backwards, count, how many...?, round, square, size, order

Your child will be learning to talk about shapes.

Read the rhyme to your child pointing out the shapes in the pictures.

What's the Shape?

Here's a **circle** curved and round,

Draw it big and touch the ground,

Round and round and round it goes,

Make it small upon my nose.

Triangles have 3 straight sides,

I've made mine so big and wide,

Lots of them are in the air,

I can see them at the fair.

Rectangles have 4 straight sides,

Draw them all so tall and wide,

Make the sides now all the same,

Call it by another name!

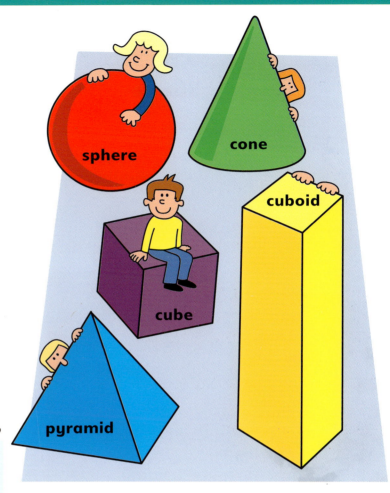

sphere

cone

cuboid

cube

pyramid

Read the rhyme again with your child, but this time draw the shapes in the air as you read it.

A rectangle with 4 sides all the same length is a square. ('Rectangle' means that the shape has right angles of 90 degrees).

The pictures show the 4 shapes in the rhyme in different sizes and orientations. Help your child to find all the different triangles, circles, rectangles and squares.

You will also be able to find some solid shapes like bricks. Those with rectangular sides are cuboids. There is also a cube, a cone, a sphere (ball), and a pyramid.

Your child doesn't need to know the names of the shapes yet, but some children really like learning new names. Being able to describe shapes by talking about straight or curved sides, the number of sides, and whether it is big or small is much more important than knowing the names of the shapes at this stage.

MORE THINGS TO TRY

Spinning Shapes

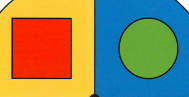

You need: lots of counters of 2 kinds (e.g. different coloured/shaped buttons), and a pencil and paper clip to work the spinner.

Rules:

1. Take turns to spin the 'shape spinner' and remember your shape e.g. circle.
2. Spin the 'size spinner' and remember your size e.g. small.
3. Now cover the small circle with your counter.
4. Sometimes there won't be a shape of your kind free so you miss that turn.
5. The winner is the one who has the most counters on the page at the end of the game.

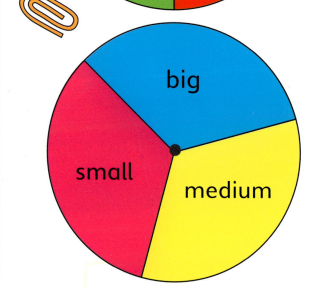

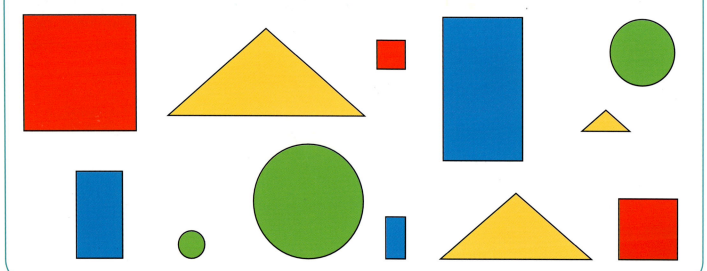

Find patterns around the house (e.g. on clothes, furniture) and talk about these with your child. Repeat the patterns below with your child:

Blue, red, blue, red, blue. What colour comes next?

> *It really helps to say the patterns out loud (e.g. car, teddy, car, teddy, car). Your child will hear the pattern and then will be able to join in with you.*

Make some repeating patterns with toys or coloured crayons, or by threading beads. Include complex ones such as bowl, spoon, spoon, bowl, spoon, spoon, bowl.

1.

2.

Keep counting! • • • • • • • • • • • •

• Count to 100 by rote with your child. Count in tens (10, 20, 30, etc.) to 50, and when your child is confident with this, count in tens to 100. You can do what is done in schools and hold up all 10 fingers for a moment as you count, so you hold them up 10 times to reach a 100.

> *When you count in ones to 100 your child is likely to say '20 10' instead of 30, but will catch onto the pattern of the numbers if you keep repeating them together.*

• Do some 'sound counting'. Drop some coins into a tray, one at a time, so that they make a noise. Ask your child to count them as you drop them. Make it harder by dropping the coins (with his back turned) at irregular intervals to see if the counting stays accurate. This is hard!

Maths fun!

Hunt the Toy

Rules:

1. Hide a small toy when your child is out of the room.
2. Ask him to find the toy. Give him clues using the language of position e.g. 'It is under something blue', 'It is next to a large box', 'It is behind your favourite teddy', etc.

Maths words

cuboid, rectangular, cube, cone, sphere, circle, rectangle, big, round, small, straight, wide, tall, curved, triangle, square, guess

Your child will be learning to read and trace numbers to 10.

1 2 3 4 5
6 7 8 9 10

Read the rhyme a few times to your child, pointing to the numbers as you go.

Honey Buns

No buns in the bag, not a single bun,
Put one in and make it 1.

1 bun in the bag, that's too few,
Add another one and make it 2.

2 buns in the bag, one for you and me,
Add another one and make it 3.

3 buns in the bag, let's buy more,
Add another one and make it 4.

4 buns in the bag, mind that hive!
Add another one and make it 5.

5 buns in the bag, hey, no licks,
Add another one and make it 6.

6 buns in the bag, on the way to Devon,
Add another one and make it 7.

7 buns in the bag, let's jump the gate,
Add another one and make it 8.

8 buns in the bag, how many are mine?
Add another one and make it 9.

9 buns in the bag, let's run and then,
Add another one and make it 10.

10 buns in the bag, shared by you and me,
Let's sit down and have some tea!

You need: 10 'buns' (bricks or play dough) and a paper bag.

Read the rhyme again, but this time introduce a 'bun' into each verse. Stop to talk about how many buns there are in each verse:

How many do we have now? Can you find that number on the page? How many will we have if we add one more?

When you have counted 8 buns in the bag, ask your child to share them out between you. Then do the same with 10 buns.

Sharing can be done with the 'one for you, one for me' method. Formal division isn't learnt until children are about age 7.

There are 12 buzzy bees to count on this page and there are 12 more hiding in the book for your child to find.

MORE THINGS TO TRY

Starting with 10 fingers, fold them down one by one and say:

I'm holding up 10 fingers. If I fold one down, how many are left standing up? If I fold down another one, how many will there be?

Keep counting! . . . .

Guess How Many?

Rules:

1. **Put 5 raisins on a plate and ask your child to guess how many there are.**
2. **Then count them together.**
3. **Repeat this with a different number of raisins.**
4. **Ask your child to match a number card (from page 5) with the objects.**

When there are a large number of objects, your child might just say that there are lots! Gradually help to extend this idea by asking him whether there are more than 20, more than 50 or is it nearer to a 100. Making guesses (or estimating) is important because at school your child will need to know how to estimate or 'make a good guess'.

Remember that children often love large numbers. You might not want to get dragged into counting how many raisins in a packet, but if you can stand it, it might be fun!

What's the Number, Mr Mouse?

Rules:
1. Put the number cards (from page 5) in a bag and pick one out at a time saying the number in a little mouse voice.
2. Turn over the card and count the dots. Slow him down if he is counting too fast.
3. If your child needs extra support count out the same number of buttons as dots on the card.
4. Extend the game by asking your child to put the number in his head and then count on the number of dots on the back of the card to total 10 e.g. the number 4 card has 6 dots on the back, so ask your child to put 4 in his head and count on 6 dots to get 10.

Note that the dots are arranged in dice and domino patterns. It is helpful if your child can recognise those patterns quickly and knows, for example, ⚅ *is 6.*

Maths fun!

Play the 'Race to the Fair' game on page 4, but with different rules:

You need: lots of counters for each player (e.g. coins, buttons, raisins), and a pencil and paper clip to work the spinner.

Rules:
1. Start with a counter each on the house.
2. Take turns to spin the spinner and move one of your counters that many spaces. If you land on a red star, move your counter to the end and then on your next go you can start with another of your counters.
3. If you land on a blue circle, that counter has to go back to the start.
4. If you land on a green triangle, you can move that counter straight to the end as well as one of your other counters .
5. The winner is the first to get 10 counters to the end (or a lower number for a quicker game).

Variation: play the game on page 4 making up your own rules!

Maths words
another, how many...?, share, guess, estimate, count, too few, fewer, add, one more

See What I Can Do!

I can talk about these shapes.

I know what comes next in this pattern.

I know these numbers.

Listen to how far I can count!

I can put number cards in order.

I can count backwards.

  8 7 6 5 4 3 2 1 0

There are 5 raisins altogether.
I know how many are hiding.

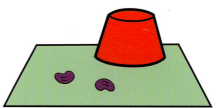

I can write some numbers.

I can count in tens; 10, 20, 30, 40...

I found 12 Buzzy Bees in this book.